A SMALL MIRACLE

PETER COLLINGTON

For dear Mum

A Red Fox Book

Published by Random House Children's Books
20 Vauxhall Bridge Road, London SW1V 2SA
A division of Random House UK Ltd
London Melbourne Sydney Auckland
Johannesburg and agencies throughout the world

1 3 5 7 9 10 8 6 4 2

First published in Great Britain by Jonathan Cape 1997

Red Fox edition 1999

Printed in Hong Kong by Midas Printing Ltd

RANDOM HOUSE UK Limited Reg. No. 954009

ISBN 0 09 968071 8

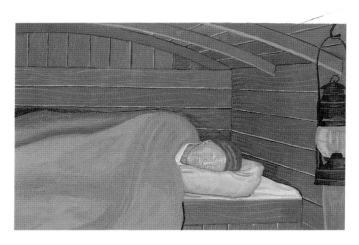
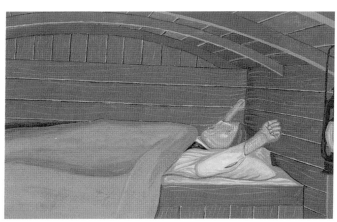

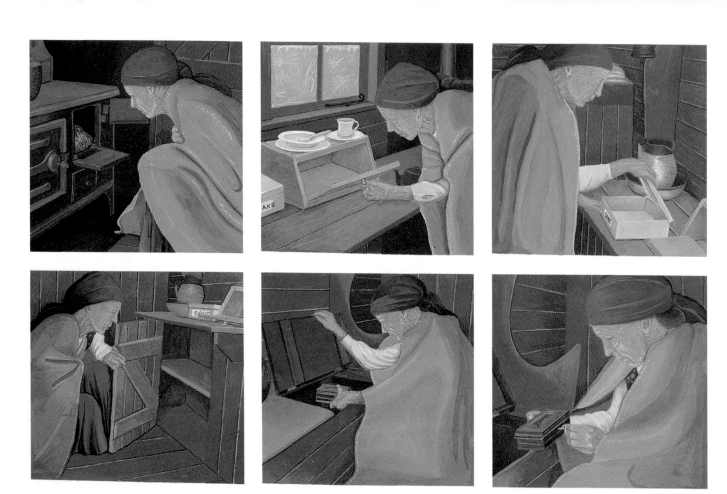

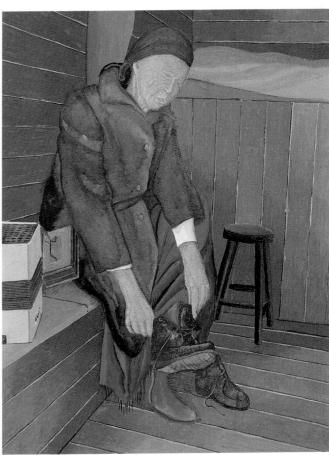

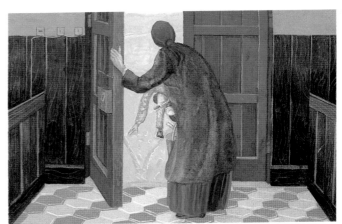

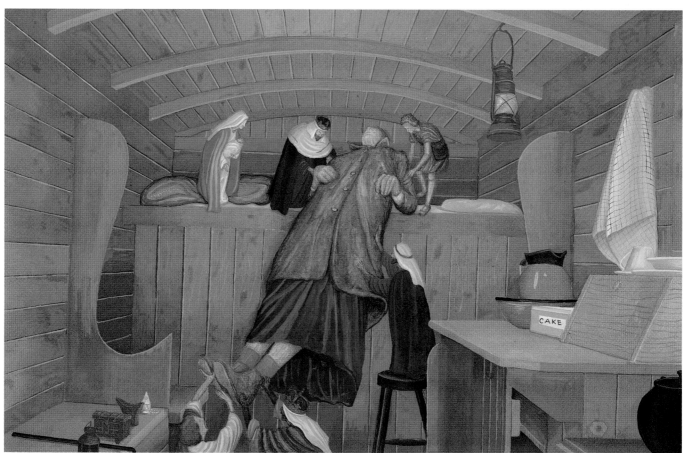

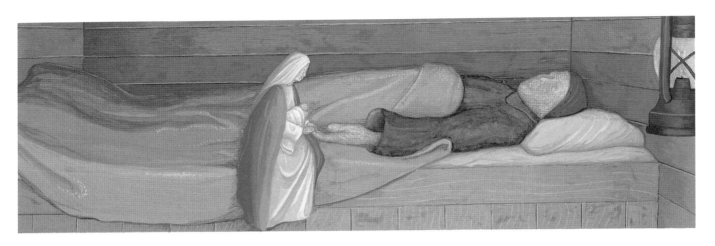

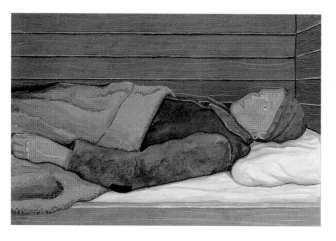